The Angry Fighter's Story

The Angry Fighter's Story

Harness the Fire Within

Bill Vincent

Published by Revival Waves of Glory Books & Publishing

PO Box 596| Litchfield, Illinois 62056 USA

www.revivalwavesofgloryministries.com

Revival Waves of Glory Books & Publishing is committed to excellence in the publishing industry.

Published in the United States of America

Paperback: 978-1684111510

Hardcover: 978-1684111527

Table of Contents

Chapter One:

In the Beginning

I take the steps two at a time, these was as far as my legs could go. From behind me, I hear the sounds of hot pursuit and the piggish tones of Tom the nasty as we call him and the hoots that was the trademark of his gang. Heart pounding, I reach the top of the stairs and make a beeline for the stack of abandoned boxes in the hallway. They had been in use once and had fallen out of favour with the passage of time. They had been earmarked for disposal by the refuse truck when it came around and I guess no one had gotten around to moving them downstairs the zillion times since then that the truck had come around.

Trembling, I reach the relative safety of the boxes and squeezing through a small gap between it and the wall; I enter my safe place, a fortress, as I imagined it to be. To me, it was worth more than the lovely yellow flowers that sprout in spring or the tinkle that the ice makes as we play with it on ice days at the workshop. Although, it could not take the place of a warm plate of chocolate, steaming delicately on a wooden table with a spoon clutched between my fingers.

Oddly enough, that is a memory that comes from a cloudy past, a time before I came into the home for boys and…

Oh! My name is David Hunter. At least that is the name the matron told me I bore and her word is law around here. I guess she would have no reason to lie but I am aware, in fact, we are aware of the fact that she is a consummate liar. Over a thousand stories of legends exist *(only a few really, only that they got bolder with each retelling)*, told by boys in hushed voices at night after lights out, tales finely woven with just enough yarn and garnished with enough childish fantasy to capture our imagination.

The city we were in I learnt was Chicago and that was what the older boys who knew about many things said it was called. This they claimed to have seen on a thing called a map. What that means, I have no idea.

In the truly miserable periods, when the older boys become nasty and seize my food, I often wonder where I came from. The matron says I had been dropped at the door of the home in a basket with soft blankets wrapped around me. Attached to it was an envelope, which said, *"Please keep him safe, someone will come for him eventually."*

I was told that years ago and nobody ever came. Some of the boys were adopted some were claimed by their families and others were taken to states for a big sounding program or the other but no one ever came for me.

I was of a somewhat slight build through these years. Perhaps on the scrawnier side but this could have been because we rarely had enough to eat throughout the year except during the holidays and religious festivals when we got a lot of gifts and the state officials felt satiated enough to send the full allocation to the homes. I remember always being hungry. It became a normal part of my life, a gnawing emptiness that never filled and was perpetually awake.

Boys are troublesome enough without hunger being added to the equation and its presence sometimes made life at the home horrible. I got beat up a lot and had my food seized by ravenous tigers (older boys), ignored and not picked at games because I was too scrawny and was often compared to a plucked chicken by my mates.

We had loads of free time and we spent it on the streets of Chicago, at times with errands to run, most often without the permission and knowledge of the home staff of which we had three. Old Sam who was the security guard, janitor, handy man, workshop mentor and so many other jobs rolled into one. We had the Matron who was the general. She commands the house and wields the iron spoon, this apparatus was one she wielded with accuracy and we were all afraid of being on the receiving end of it as it delivered some nasty discipline and dished out pain in generous quantities. Lastly, there is Abe. She was the cook, laundry woman and teacher.

A face peers through a gap in the boxes at the edge of my vision and I barely register this, as I was deep in thought. There came whispers from around the pile of boxes and this gets my attention. I leap to my feet in fear with chills running down my spine.

"They have found me" I thought despairingly and attempt to flee before they discover the gap that was the way in. I squeezed against the wall and was cautiously sidling through the gap when a fist comes out of nowhere and grabs me by the scruff of the neck.

Terrified, I began to struggle and kick as hard as I could but the grip only tightens and I am dragged inexorably out of the gap to face the beating of a lifetime. I am beaten almost every day but this feels like it was going to be much worse.

It was.

I was pummelled badly. I opened my eyes to see a fist flying towards my face and from then on, it was a kaleidoscope of pain. Tom and his whole gang beat me gleefully. I had mixed some bird poo with my lunch and they mixed it with theirs after they seized it from me. What gave me away was the big grin on my face as I watched them gobble up with gusto, this and the fact that Mat, a member of the gang had once worked at a poultry and knew what bird poo smelled like.

They were very mad and immediately came for me.

Now, as I lie coiled into a ball on the floor, powerless and defenceless, as the blows descend on my body, blood pours from a gash in my brow from the buckle of a shoe as the after effect of a kick to the head. A slow burning starts in my heart, a disgust at being unable to do a thing to protect myself coupled with the belief that the world is very unfair.

A sharp pain erupts suddenly in my stomach, as a kick somehow evades the defensive cover of my arms and connects solidly with the soft flesh of my tummy. The pain sprouts in a sharp rictus, rising in intensity until I convulse and cry out overwhelmed by the agony. The blows immediately stop at my cry and a voice cries out in a hushed voice, *"What have we done?"*

There is silence for a few moments and then another voice says, *"I wasn't here."*

The sound of running feet follows the voice and then like clockwork, the gang scatters all around me headed in different directions.

This is all I remember as the darkness closes in around me. It takes away the pain and I float into a comforting emptiness.

Sunlight spills in through white curtained windows and its rays splash teasingly across the face of a brown haired boy, heavily bandaged and wearing a hospital gown.

I open my eyes to a brilliantly white room and it hurts to keep my eyes open just for a while. There is a woman sitting by the bed and before slipping back into the darkness, I catch a whisper, as it twirls slowly in my consciousness as I drift back down.

"*You are going to be all right David; this I promise you.*"

Chapter Two

The days quietly flit by and I get better in steady increments. I had been in a very bad state when I arrived at the hospital. The doctors had been quite horrified at the extent of bodily damage I had sustained during the assault and had rightly called the cops. As a result, the state sent investigators to the home for boys and their findings caused such a stir that the state caused all welfare homes for both the poor, orphans and every other special needs to be investigated and their accounts audited.

Skeletons began to emerge from musty cupboards and the scandal that literally hit the roof was one of the worst the state had ever had. Officials were demoted, some sacked out rightly and a host of others were transferred to new duty posts. I lay in the Intensive Care Unit all this while, unaware of the tornado my ordeal at the hands of a group of playground bullies had caused. According to the doctor's report, I had three heavily bruised ribs, a swollen wrist joint, a mild concussion and an ankle sprain. My eyes were also almost swollen shut with bruises and I couldn't see distinctly at all for the first few days.

It was on one of those days that I had woken up to my aunt's presence. All I had perceived had been through the bandages my eyes were swaddled in. I had been slipping in and out of consciousness even back then, so all I could see was a ladylike figure in a white room. Her presence at my bedside soon became familiar to me and her arrival had a soothing effect on me. Instinctively, on a subliminal level, I recognized someone who genuinely cared for me and thought of me as family. This realization I can claim, was the singular factor to my speedy recovery. I was soon shifted from intravenous sustenance to a liquid diet, then a soft fibrous liquid diet and on schedules perhaps designed by the doctor, I was soon back on a relatively normal albeit very natural and more nutritious diet.

Soon it was time for the bandages to come off and I got to see my aunt fully for the first time. We share a marked similarity; she has brown hair like mine. However, hers is of a slightly deeper shade. She has dimples and a beautiful smile. Overall, I would call her a pretty woman based on my short life experience and the fantasy of stories told by boys.

I was discharged soon after and released into the custody of my aunt who had staked her claim with the state department. Now, I sit on the couch and my heart beats fiercely against my rib cages. My fists clenched tight and my knuckles stand out from the surrounding skin. They are white and trembling with the effort of trying to drill the ground with an iron rod. Teeth clenched, I fight valiantly and tether on the edge of a wide abyss of rage.

My first week at school had been going well and I had succeeded in staying below the radar, speaking only when addressed, being polite to teachers and everything was going smoothly.

On Thursday afternoon, it was the midday break and I headed towards the cafeteria when a voice sneered from behind me, *"Hey newbie! Think you are too good to walk with us."*

I did not respond but quickened my step as the hallway suddenly seemed deserted and the nearest person to me was about to turn the corner into the cafeteria.

"Come on, slow down mate, we just want to talk."

I never looked back until I reached the cafeteria and trudged to join the queue that was moving slowly. The anger I had assumed gone was back. It had risen with the fear coupled with the anxiety of being attacked again and the thought of going through the suffering I had been subjected to further fuelled the rage at being forced to cower and made to walk this path again. I finished my meal and went looking for them.

I never found them. I marched back to class and at the edges of my vision, I could see students giving me a little berth, I guess my expression must have been thunderous. Since I had not seen the faces of the guys who had challenged me, I could not really identify them and none of my classmates held my gaze till the end of that school day. I went home, irritable and angry.

The next day was Friday. I had been pressed and had obtained permission from the History teacher. He had been droning on for about 50 minutes and about half of the class were dozing on their seats. He was however unperturbed and continued his monologue about the third amendment or something (*I stopped listening a while ago*).

The hallways were deserted and the male toilets were down the hall. I snuck my hands into my pockets and strolled sedentarily. I wasn't in a hurry to get back to class and could afford to dither a little bit before re-entering that atmosphere.

Halfway down the hall, hands seized me from behind and hauled me by the scruff of the neck through a door marked Staff Only, it was under repair. There I was dumped onto the floor. Looking up at my assailants, I see that they are jocks, all three of them sporting identical team jackets with their initials or nickname stencilled on the back.

There were high fives all around and they stand grinning down at me as one of them moves and leans down slightly, towards me.

"Pretty boy, we guess you've got enough time to talk now," he quips.

With that, his cohorts burst into another round of laughter and the flood steadily builds up along my chest and up my throat.

When I did not give a response, another of them moves closer and smirking stretches his hand to prod me in the chest with a finger while looking back towards his friends. *"Let's see if he can talk…"*

The world around me explodes and everything turns red. My anger flashes into rage and passes the breaking point. I grab his finger and twist it sharply. He yowls terribly in pain and I think I hear a creak from somewhere. Letting go of his hand, he scuttles back whimpering and I turn to face the others. A blow is headed towards my face. It seems to move too slowly and I have no problem sidestepping it. It misses and I reply with a fist to the guts. He loses his breath with a big *whoosh* and crumples to the ground, groaning weakly.

All fired up now, I turned to face the last one. As I approach, he raises his arms towards me in surrender and there is fear written all over his face. I stop, struck by the familiarity of his gesture and the teachers come running in.

So here I am.

I throw the iron rod away in disgust and walk back into the living room, there I pace the room restlessly. I am waiting for my aunt to get back from her meeting with the counsellor. The two teachers were coming in from a science conference they had attended, when the cry of pain had alarmed them. The fact that the sound came from an abandoned toilet under repairs doubled their fears.

A single glance told the story and while one takes the groaning boys to the infirmary, the other teacher takes the last one and I to the Counsellor's office. Strangely, the boy was sternly reprimanded as I was too but I got the feeling that mine was handled delicately. The disciplinary council then called my aunt and arranged for a staff to drop me off at home while she attended the meeting.

Frustrated and still angry, my pacing becomes even more restless and a persistent itch develops on my scalp. Walking quickly, the urge to punch something grows until I can't resist. Barely holding on, I leave the living room and move into the hallway (*can't afford breaking any of my aunt's beloved decorative china*).

A door I have never seen opened stands to my left and it draws in my anger. I punch the door with all my might and it reverberates with the force of the blow. My hand explodes in pain and throbs with red-hot pulses. The anger, however, is now a little stream, satiated and expended.

As I turn to go find some ice for my hand in the fridge, a click comes from behind me. The door slowly swings open with the hinges protesting lightly as it does. I turn back and stand there, awestruck.

A floor to ceiling poster stares back at me. On it is a well-built and equally proportioned specimen of a man. He has red boxing gloves on his hands, his smile is confident and his eyes hold the promise of adventure and a steely determination.

The inscription below it reads *"Frank Lightening"*.

Tearing my eyes from the picture as the door comes to a halt against the wall affording me a better view of the room; the walls are covered with posters of all sizes of the same man. There is a table piled high with tapes and in a corner stands a shelf with colourful robes, and another shelf to the side holds an assortment of things that I cannot identify and this is all I can see from my vantage point in the hallway before the open door.

As I curiously crane my neck to see more of the room, a horn beeps twice from outside the house and my heart leaps in my throat.

My aunt is back and that is her signal to come help with her shopping or whatever else she brought home with her. Hurriedly, I pull shut the door while trying to prevent its rusted hinges from creaking.

Wiping my sweaty hands on my pants, I then rush out to meet my aunt.

Chapter Three

You can't hide things from family they say. I guess I should have known that this would probably ring true. My aunt made no mention of the meeting at my school. She warmly replied to my greeting and her behaviour was not in any way changed as we went through the motions of the evening routine, preparing dinner, checking the bills, arranging the laundry and doing the chores that accompanied our arrival at home after a busy weekday.

The moment I had been dreading did come but it was not totally as I expected. I was sitting on the sofa in the living room with a writing board on my lap, trying to do some school assignments when she called me from the hallway.

"David, come over here." Her tone was strange. It had an odd quality to it and seemed to catch but this I reasoned with only part of my mind while the major part quaked silently as I stood and putting the writing board to the side, walked towards her gingerly like a man that's about to be slain.

Her next words catch me by surprise and for a few moments, I stand with literally one foot in the air and my mouth open like a fish wondering how on Earth she had gotten to know.

The statement was phrased like a question but sounded more like a statement of fact, *"You opened this door."*

Eventually, I find my voice and reply, *"Yes I did, it was not intentional though and I punched the door accidentally."*

At my reply, her eyebrows rose a fraction and I had the grace to look away, at anything but her.

"You were angry, weren't you?" she asked quietly, with concern etching her voice and I nod in acquiescence. She considers me for a few moments and then sighing, pushes upon the door.

"You might as well as come in and meet him since you have already seen him," she says as she enters the room with her skirt swishing gently behind her.

With trembling legs and an increasing pulse, I step into the room.

"My husband Frank was a fighter," she says as she gently traces the contours of the poster I had seen earlier with the tips of her fingers. *"He was one of the best. I lost him some years ago and since then, there has been no one to use his stuff and I packed them in here."*

Turning to me, I can see tears glistening in her eyes. *"You all I have and family must stick together. I understand that you have gone through a lot and Frank also had some issues at a stage in his life, but boxing helped give him a new perspective. Go through his stuff, watch his videos and make your decision. Whatever you say, I will always be here for you but promise me one thing, never to fight in school or anywhere you could get in trouble with the law.*

With tears now running down my face, I nod and smiling warmly, she envelopes me in a hug and there we stand for some time.

The next day at school, the guys who I fought with in the toilet came to meet me in the company of two other friends in the cafeteria. As soon as I set my eyes on them, the anger came roaring back along with the memories and I was stunned by its intensity and how powerful it was. Remembering that I had given my word and personally not looking to start a fight, I fought furiously to regain control of my emotions. Sitting there rigidly, and every muscle in my body tense, I struggled imperceptibly for some seconds with only a few twitches of my brow giving the indication that anything was wrong.

I am barely aware of the polite requests to sit down that the group now standing beside me made. I painstakingly wrest control back and push the boiling rage back until it longer threatened to spill over and there it quietened down for the time being. Breathing a bit heavily now, I visibly relax and nod curtly at the jocks to have a seat.

The first thing they did was to apologize and as far as I could tell, their apology was genuine. As Jimmy (*they introduced themselves, he was the guy I punched in the stomach*) succinctly put it, *"We never meant to hurt you man, we just wanted to have some harmless fun with the new guy and just push him around a little. There was no way we could have guessed that you are sensitive to such things and have had horrible experiences. We are sorry for all you have gone through and the little we might have added to it."*

I nod and reply, *"It's okay, no hard feelings, just don't come on people too strongly. You cannot know how they might react or what they have been through and bullying even if it's just for the fun of it is also wrong."*

A cloud visibly lifts from their faces, bodies and postures. I had not noticed how tense they too were, not until that point. I am guessing someone at the counsellor's office probably told them my story. We soon got to talking and they introduced themselves. I soon found out that we had quite a few things in common and I enjoyed the company *(been getting tired of being lonely and eating alone).*

My days soon take on a something of a regular pattern. Getting back from school, I would eat and then rush to the boxing room *(that's what I now call it)* to watch the tapes of my uncle's moves and before long, I was mimicking his every move while imagining what it was like to be in his shoes. Most times, I would study the large poster, studying every line and definition of his muscles and imagining what it was like to punch someone with such power and force. Along with these thoughts came the storm that was my anger and the almost irresistible urge to punch or break something. It was borne at the idea of the unfairness of life, the parents I never knew, the home I never had, the experiences I endured and the amazing uncle I never met.

On some days, the pressure was so great that I would slip on a pair of gloves and proceed to hammer the bag hung in a corner of the room (*some would call it a punching bag but I didn't know what it was called*). It was on one of such evenings that my aunt peeped into the room and caught sight of the venom laden blows I was gifting the punching bag. She didn't try to get my attention but brought up the issue at dinner that night.

"How would you like to start training professionally to be a boxer? It would be a great help to you and help you become a better person."

I nod enthusiastically in reply and the matter was settled.

My aunt arrived from work very early the next day, just a few minutes after I arrived from school. After getting into the car with her, we soon arrive at a modest gym, which was a considerable distance from the house.

As soon as we enter, the smell of canvas, plastic and sweat hits me and the combination is organic. My aunt leaves me to go find someone and I look around. There are equipment of every size and shape whose function I could not fathom and countless punching bags. These also differed in sizes and some were arranged one after the other in a form.

"Hello, you must be David. I am Mark, and I was your uncle's trainer. Your aunt here has told me about me, and she says you

might just be as good as he was. So boy, you ready?"

At first glance, he is muscular, impressively so with a wide chest and nice biceps but his smile is open and welcoming, his eyes also twinkle with mirth, unconsciously, and I relax and reflect on what he has said.

"This here is real, it involves hard work, determination, consideration, empathy (yes, empathy), perseverance and the greatest of all is faith and never dying belief, so what do you say?" he completes while stretching his hand out towards me.

I stretch out my hand and clasp his proffered hand and his grip is strong but he makes sure it doesn't hurt me. He pats me on the shoulder as I stand beside him, then pulling me by the arm; he begins to show me around the gym.

A quiet feeling floats up in my heart and it rings true as I walk through the gym behind Mark.

"I am home and it feels like home."

Chapter Four

Mark must have been pushing close to fifty. Heck, he could even have been years older than that, my guess was based on a rough estimation of his looks and, boy, was I wrong! A few days after I began training with Mark at the gym, a couple of old geezers came by the gym (*pardon the pun but they were very wrinkled, almost ancient*). From the greetings, it was clear to me that they were highly regarded by everyone at the gym. So imagine my shock when about three of them addressed Mark as old pal with peculiar hugs and special greeting styles that characterize old friends.

They chat amiably for some time before Mark beckons to me from where I have been running on a spot (*yeah, he calls it cooling down*).

As I approach them, I catch the tail end of their conversation. "*…. he is a kid I just took on; you know I retired but Marge, Frank's sweetie, convinced me that he has it and since I was bored of doing nothing and my kids have been badgering to come down to New Orleans….*" Here, he visibly shudders and the others shake their head in sympathy. He is about to continue when I reach them dripping in sweat from head to toe (*hadn't even guessed I could ever sweat this much*).

"Oh, meet David, everyone," he says and I accept proffered handshakes from all. None of them seemed to mind my sweaty palms and the moisture covering my hands. They all grasped my hand and somewhat manfully *(won them points in my book).* I learnt they mostly had been boxers and trainers who had known my uncle. They had trained and worked their careers during his era and all had glowing recollections of his bouts and how he was in the ring.

"He was real lightening to watch." One called Paul says, *"He earned that name by ending about seven consecutive bouts within the first twenty seconds. He would knock out his opponent within that time and they would not make the countdown. Can you just imagine the power of the blows that it took to achieve that and all in the first round, where*

stamina and strength are considered full and at optimal levels?"

They leave soon after but their words never fade and my heart swells with big dreams but as the saying goes *"If wishes were horses…"* I was now at the stage of discovering new muscles and places I did not know I could feel pain in. I must admit to having been surprised and then shocked. On the second day after I met Mark, I had been anticipating a whirlwind sought of training, delving into fight patterns, tricks and insights into the world of boxing.

Well, that was exactly what happened if you look at it from the opposite spectrum. I spent that day at a logging station hoisting planks and almost all shapes and sizes of wood except perhaps the biggest that were handled with machinery. A small comfort should probably be the fact that he worked as I worked and was still cool and dry by the time I was puffing and huffing at midday.

Taking pity on me, he called a rest and I just about collapsed on the ground to the amusement of the mill workers. Mark had an arrangement with them with regards to training and they treated the sight of us working alongside them as normal. Well, the next weeks were not really much of an improvement. I did not even get to see much of the insides of the gym, only met up with Mark there before he hustled us out and onwards to the next training plan, he had concocted.

I would run behind his truck while being tied to it, as he would drive at what he called a snail's pace. We would transverse the whole district with everyone calling out greetings to Mark. *"You have got a new one."* They would say, *"Keep it up young man."* And I kept it up, through the morning, and afternoons on weekends and evenings on weekdays, jogging until I was exhausted and shaking from head to foot.

And Mark would stride out from the truck after each lap clutching his stopwatch, *"You can still do better, young man, much better."* And little by little, my frustration grew bit-by-bit and transposed into a dull anger awaking the old nemesis. The straw that broke the camel's back came quite innocuously one afternoon.

"I have a surprise for you," he had said that afternoon while grinning widely. I

had just got back from school and after resting a little bit had made my way to the gym to meet up with him. After a few minutes' drive, he turned into a ranch driveway and I was nonplussed, what now?

As it turned out, my training for the afternoon was to catch well-oiled pigs (*the oiling was an arrangement with the farm owners, I guess*) but the sorting was normal farm procedure to group those within the same size and growth range. For about half an hour, I succeeded in catching (*you guessed it*) nothing! In relation, the farm hands caught about twenty pigs each.

Frustrated, I finally turn to Mark and explode. *"Am fed up man, what more can I do to convince you to teach me? All you have been doing is toying with me and just having fun at my expense. If am not worth your time, please say so and I will leave you in peace."* I finish in a towering rage and shaking with emotion.

He laughs in response and I stare at him in consternation and disbelief.

Wiping his eyes, he finally replies, *"Been waiting for you to show some spirit and backbone. You sounded almost like your uncle and that is the spark I have been waiting for."*

Seeing that I was still mad, he raises his hands in a placating gesture. *"I know all we have been doing doesn't really seem like much but I assure you that our training has not been just for the fun of it. Each one was picked to strengthen a particular area, the jogging is designed to strengthen your joints, increase your stamina and energy, the saw mill to give you raw strength and power while building up your muscle density and padding which helps absorb blows, this pig farm is to improve your reflexes, reaction time and heighten your awareness."*

Drawing me closer, he holds me at arm length and says, *"I see great potential in you and gave you my word to be your trainer, that, I don't take lightly. You have shown all that I require and even more, so now we will begin the next phase of your training starting at the gym tomorrow."*

The atmosphere in the gym the next day was palpable. I could literally feel the energy zapping through the air. There was an air of expectation and everyone greeted me with a nod and a smile.

"Good luck kid," they all said, in one way or the other and as I made my way from the locker room into the gym proper, I soon saw why. Mark had a small stage set up and a board with records was the centrepiece. Each of these records covered a particular part of the gym facility set by boxers who used the equipment and a small banner to the side, pronounced me as Davie challenging the existing records.

Naturally, I was freaked out but Mark soon had me grounded with a few words, *"This is what you want to do, smashing these is along the path to achieving your dreams and even if you don't, we will know where you are and where we need to work on in getting you ready for your first fight."*

I nod and steel myself. The first was a punching bag on a slider, the force of a punch should propel it along the rail ruler. As I face it, the anger comes welling and I let go of control, open the floodgates and out it poured.

I smash my fist into the bag and it squeaks down the slide with the force of the blow. There are excited murmurs as the measurements are taken and some whispers float up to me, *"… he is quite strong for his age… "*

It was a record but only for my weight grade. I was nowhere near the gym record for the sheer power of a blow. The next was the treadmill and here I shattered all records, setting new sprint records, long distance records and the staggered lap records. Mark grins at me like a Cheshire cat from his seat near the boxing ring when the results were announced. Speed boxing was next and it involves consistently punching a spring like punching ball hanging from the roof that rebounds with every blow. My hands began aching long before I could no longer continue, so that record is safe for now. Throughout the rest of the afternoon, I am tested with and put through a wide range of equipment I cannot describe and break only a couple more records.

As I limp up the stairs that night, Mark calls after me, *"You are ready for your first fight mate. Although, we are keeping small, it's just an indoor gym bout with one of the established guys; it is fixed for next Saturday."* Then making a turn in the street, he zooms off.

And I limp up the rest of the stairs with a wildly skipping heart and fire coursing through my veins.

"Yeah! Bring it on!"

Chapter Five

I sit very still, muscles tight and back ramrod straight. I hardly move at all, even the ones taken to breath are hardly noticeable. An observer from a neutral perspective would be forgiven for thinking I was a Mannequin. The class is silent as the teacher collects the sheets for the test and he then leaves the class. The anger is back and along with it comes a feeling of insecurity and shaky nerves. The cause, my first fight is tomorrow and I am freaking out.

My relationship with my classmates has changed over the past months as I train with Mark. I learn confidence, patience, perseverance and a host of other virtues from him. He would sit me down about three times a week after our training sessions and we would have long discussions, which I enjoyed and soon began actively looking forward to. He became a sort of uncle-figure for me and I got to ask a lot of questions I had previously been unable to ask my aunt, especially those about girls and the feelings I sometimes had (*Come on, it's true, don't roll your eyes*).

Unconsciously, my appearance improved. I now paid more attention to what I wore and how my hair looked. One of Mark's favourite saying was *"to be respected, you have to first look respectable.”* I no longer looked so scrawny and soon had soft rounded developments proportionally all over my body. When at first I noticed especially those on my stomach called packs, I was bubbling over to show Mark and he just shook his head and pulling his shirt up, showed me his. I was totally floored and was hit with the realization that I had quite a long way to go.

My improved appearance and much relaxed expression must have made me more approachable as I soon began receiving smiles in the hallways, which I tentatively returned. I was pleasantly surprised when on an afternoon; I was invited to join a group of friends at their table in the cafeteria. Much later, they confided in me that unlike before when I was withdrawn, coiled tight, head lowered and not wishing to be approached, I was now open, head raised, alert and likable. Hearing this did much for my confidence and I told Mark who was pleased at how well I was adapting.

However, there was one thing that did not change. All it did was become dull during periods and then flare when I was provoked. Although I was able to keep from lashing out on several occasions and keep a tight lid on things, I was still as volatile as ever. As the days went by and my first fight draws closer, I become touchy, anxious and sometimes border on the edge of panic and as all situations too close to fire are prone to do, I soon burst into flames.

I had arrived that morning to find that my combination lock had been tampered with and some notes had been stolen. This fuelled a dull anger that did not abate till the class test later in the day. My anger increased as the test we did was based on the stolen note. I was unable to revise and all I had to go with was a shady recollection. As soon as the teacher left the class, I hurriedly stood and left the class to get some fresh air and clear my head.

Well, let's just say I never had the opportunity. I turn around a corner and descend the stairs. Turning left, I spy sudden movement from the edges of my vision and turn to see two figures struggling with a slight figure between them as they disappear down a dark corner. Running swiftly, I turn the corner and enter an abandoned classroom and there, two guys had a third pinned against the wall and one held his hands up while the others rained blows on him.

I literally see red having been in such situations as this. My rage frightens even me. Roaring in fury, I charge at them and taking one look at me, they both blanch and drop the little guy (*guess my face must have been quite thunderous*). Licking their lips, they both stand shoulder to shoulder as I charge them within a split second, time slows down to a crawl, everything moves slowly and little movements seem stretched out. At the last second, one of the guys attempts to bolt and without thinking, I stretch out a foot, trip him and he crashes to the floor. The other then squares up to me. He swings and I sidestep his wild swing. It's totally lacking power, its trajectory is wide and it pushes him off-balance. He somehow manages to right himself and sends out a left hook. Smiling wickedly now, I dodge into the curve of his arms and his entire torso is left unprotected before me, ripe and ready for some punishment.

As in a replay, Mark's words come to mind as my punch travels through the air, "…*Don't overly commit but switch your weight from the left to right foot, transferring power up from your toes, through your torso, up your shoulders and into your arms. Your whole body follows through and you readjust as you connect, on your toes and ready to dart away from the next….*"

I let out a breath as my blows land, a quick left right combination placed below the ribs on a soft wad of muscles (*I didn't want to cause serious damage, just a little bruising as lesson).* I do not know my own strength as despite pulling the blows, the guy cries out in pain and crumples to the ground, groaning deeply and clutching his side and I stand there, with ears ringing and time speeds up again.

A little while later, I leave the Counsellor's office. I was released on the account of the little guy who was being assaulted, testified I was only defending him. As I leave, the two guys were being reprimanded. I guess they would be handed stiff punishment, since the school now frowns at all forms of bullying. Despite the exhilaration I feel, my anger does not dissipate and it instead solidifies into a dense cloud, heavy and dark.

The next day, Mark picks me up in his van and we drive to the venue of my first fight. Although he claims it was just a little thing, the venue is a popular one and I was billed to fight before the main event of the night. Mark took me through a couple of warmups and then I had my gloves bandaged on and I am outfitted in my full gear for inspection by the match official who also tells us the rules. Then, it was on to sitting in the dressing room while other matches went on. I have a bad case of jitters and soon the lights over the doors turns green and it is pulled open from behind and the door sentry says, *"It is time."*

Mark hands me my robe and I belt it around my waist. He pats me on the back and says, *"I believe in you. This is what you have been waiting for, focus and concentrate."*

We walk through a muted hallway and suddenly, come out through a doorway and into an arena emblazoned with lights. As we appear, a light turns on us, it's blinding and as Mark's hand gently pushes me from behind to continue moving, the announcer booms out, *"Introducing Davie Boy Hunter, the newest fighter to grace this hall, weighing…."*

From there, I no longer pay any attention as I am swamped by the sights and sounds. Everything becomes jumbled together, the introduction, the unrobing, the checking of gloves, and the announcement of previous fight records. Mark notices this, pulls me down and forces me to take deep breaths. *"Forget everything around us. Just focus on the fight, and everything we have done to prepare for this moment."*

I focus and the anger offers itself as support. I draw it around me like a cloak and it settles in my veins, pores, joints and muscles. The adrenalin roars through my body and I tremble with rage. I feel invincible and with the confidence of how I beat the two guys yesterday, I stand and move to the centre of the ring. Signalling our readiness, the bell rings and the first round begins.

I immediately approach him and he withdraws towards the corner, shadowing his steps. I close the distance menacingly, within striking distance, I unleash two rapid combinations and the crowd murmurs in approval. He blocks the blows and I step closer even more determined to land the first blow. Feigning a left jab, he shifts slightly and moves his hands to the right. I immediately take the opening and throw a right instead. It catches him on the side of the head and he withdraws even further into the corner, emboldened now and spurred on by the crowd who seemed to love my forwardness and raised the noise levels. I move even closer to him.

At that moment, I remember Mark's opposition analysis of that morning. *"…whatever you do, stay out of his danger zone. He lures his opponents to come closer and then springs the trap. He has a devastating right hand which is very fast…"*

As I start to move back, in sudden realization, I hear Mark's low shout, *"Get out, watch out!"*

The blow comes out of nowhere and stars burst to life in a beautiful rainbow of colours all along my vision. I see the other blow coming and raise my hands to block but my response is slow and the blow lands on my face. A hot and virulent ringing ensues around my ears and my head feels strangely light. Dimly, I hear the lines of a famous song and the sounds of sheep bleating and then everything goes dark and the last thing I remember is resting on a soft material, it's completely white and very comfortable.

Chapter Six

I sit by the window. From my position, I can see the traffic on the street, the people as they hurry home after the day's work, the happy cries of children playing with the water faucet at the corner and delightful smells drift in from the diner across the street. All this my mind dimly registers as we sit in one of the little offices in the gym complex.

"How are you feeling?" Mark asks me quietly.

How am I feeling? I think to myself, I feel horrible. It's been two days since my disastrous…Better not to think of that now, anyway it's been two days and I feel terrible and look just as bad. The left side of my face was first a bright red, and then it got swollen and slightly puffy. As of now, the puffiness and swelling are not too noticeable but the area is purplish black.

"Am fine I guess," I reply. *"What really happened to end…I can't remember?"*

Mark understands my half-spoken statement and exactly what I am asking. Leaning forward, he replies, *"Well, I guess now is a good time as any to analyse what went wrong. I loved your forwardness in the fight. It showed you were willing to take the fight to him and it's a nice trait to have. However, you failed to exercise restraint. You got carried away by the mood of the crowd, threw caution to the wind, failed to remember instructions and were too eager to force proceedings. You then moved into his danger zone and exposed yourself to his deadly right hand. He hit you with a sharp left and then his trademark right hook. To be fair to him, he was sporting enough to realize you were out of it with his second and refrained from following up with more blows. You my friend are a class act. You wavered for a few moments after his second and I began nursing hopes that you would shake it off. However, your eyes rolled up, your knees buckled, and down to the canvas, you crashed. You never even moved at all during the countdown and the fight was declared a victory for him by knockout. We got to you soon after. We meaning me, the medical team, our pals from the gym and your aunt who was unable to attend. Quite naturally, we were concerned about you being seriously hurt. But as it turned after tests, you weren't, just some bruising which were treated and you woke soon after, a little bit groggy and you know what happened from then on."*

We sit quietly as the day wears on and soon Mark says, *"We should get going, it's getting pretty late."* And we leave the gym.

On the way home in the van, Mark says, *"The fight organizers sent our cut today, we made a few hundred from our first fight despite the fact that we lost. They made us another offer and said if we were interested, we could contact them in the next few months."*

I merely nod in acknowledgement.

Soon we arrive at the house and as I get down from the van and shut the door behind me, Mark calls me back. *"Keep your head up soldier, it's not the end of the world, our greatest strength lies in not failing but in picking ourselves up and rising after every fall. See you tomorrow champ, we start training again."*

As he turns, I stand there and watch his taillights as he drives down the street and disappears around a corner. My spirits lift with his last comments and feeling much better, I turn to walk up the stairs and into the house.

However, one thing remains unchanging; the anger has now metamorphosed into red-hot rage. It strains as its bounds and I keep it caged effortlessly. I now had something to prove and a purpose for which it could be employed.

For the ensuing weeks, Mark and I return to the basics and he called in old pals who suggested friends and family for consideration as members of my team. Soon Tim came in as my Glover, and he is reputed for custom-made gloves that fit perfectly and match the fighter's preference. He was retired but was convinced by his uncle to join the team as a hobby. Mark had a cousin, Drew, who was a Physio and after brief talks, he came around one afternoon. Mark claimed he was one of the best he had ever seen and soon, after conditioning sessions with him which I ended out of breath, covered in sweat and with burning lungs, I acknowledged that he knew his stuff and he knew it cold.

Disturbed at the number of people who I now worked with, I call Mark aside one afternoon for a conversation. *"I am not too convinced by the number of people I now have to work with. I was satisfied with only you and didn't complain. I don't understand why we need a team of coaches."*

Nodding in understanding, he replies with a smile while putting an arm around my shoulders. *"Every man should know his limitations, what he is good at and the places he is gifted in. Everyone should have the courage to acknowledge the places where others are better, this is what I have done. Although I have showed you the basics of everything, the guys are specialists in their aspects and are far better teachers at it than I am as a result. Don't worry, just listen to all they say and add it to what it you know."*

The last guy to join was Mitch. He is muscular and specializes in shadow boxing, blow patterns, blow consistency and a host of other stuff. As soon as he arrived, Mark put him in charge of drilling me and armed with two blow pads, which he wears on each hand, he teaches me advanced and professional blow patterns.

About a month later, Mark finally gives in to my entreaties for us to accept the fight offer and we are billed to fight a guy who, although was a relatively new arrival on the boxing scene, already had a record of seven knockouts and two wins by unanimous decision.

I return to training with new vigour and painstakingly sharpen my rage to a gleaming point, horned for the fight.

The day arrives and we leave for the fight venue. It's the same venue, the only difference being that given the low number of fights slated for that month, we are the main event. We go through and the sights and sounds do not faze me as it had done earlier. I am focused and Mark picks up on this.

He sends me in with just a remark, *"Watch out and move, use what you have learnt."*

The bell rings and he comes at me at a furious pace. I block the blows as they come thick and fast. Gradually step by step, I give up ground until I am forced almost to the ropes with nowhere left to go. Concentrating hard, I study his blows and discover a pattern. There is a pause between his second left right combination and I exploited this. Twisting slightly for leverage, I unleash a venomous right to his midriff and he stumbles slightly, his rhythm interrupted. Warming up now, I weave to the left and then to the right as he releases short jabs and then reply with a left hook that he scrambles away from. He then cautiously shifts back and a light of grudging respect comes into his eyes. This goes straight to my head and causes me to make a fatal mistake.

The rage comes boiling up, it licks at its bounds with molten lava and I let them collapse. Adrenalin rushes through my muscles and I grin maniacally as I approach him. I feel invincible. Utilizing my longer reach, I stay out of his danger zone and begin pummelling him with short jabs, side feints and when he leaves his midriff exposed, I unleash solid blows on it.

I concentrate and utilize a right left combination, which forces him to shift, and he drops his hands for a split second. Smelling blood, I unleash direct shots at his head and as they connect, the crowd roars with approval. I forget to watch for his hands and my own vulnerability, as I follow through a particularly nasty right hook to the side of his head, his right connects with my jaw and my neck snaps painfully with the force of the blow. Disoriented and not seeing too clearly, I attempt to beat a hasty retreat and shift right into a wicked left hook. The world shudders and then turns into a thin pinprick of light, a drone zooms by overhead and then everything goes black.

Chapter Seven

I sit on the bench, the garden is deserted, flowers are scattered here and there, a little fountain gurgles quietly into the afternoon and the air is crisp, sharp and tinged with scents. The weather is pleasant, warm and the slight breeze ruffles my hair, caresses my jacket and tugs playfully at my jacket.

Through all this, the sadness does not dissipate, it is born of deep-seated gloom, a sense of shame and bleak defeat, that all I had been through had been for nothing. At that, the old rage stirs, all I do is a give it a glance and it deflates, for now. I am tired of being angry and too far-gone to care about what had made me angry in the first place.

Mark approaches from between the arch in the gardens and walks over to where I sit. We are at his friend's mansion in the country, and we came over here for the weekend. It's been two weeks since the disaster that had been my second fight and since then things have not been the same. I have stopped talking to anyone, ate only about once a day which got my aunt pretty upset and although I managed to write my final exams, I can assure you there has been no whisper of a thought carrying the tale of a valedictory ceremony.

Mark came to see me a couple of times and on these occasions, he would sit in my room with me, sometimes for hours, just sitting in silence, either reading a book or just being normal. His silence was comfortable and his presence calming. Gradually, without him saying anything, I once again began to heal and slowly, got better.

The days passed and yet, the sense of defeat persists until Mark suggests a trip out to the countryside and I accept. I didn't really have anything I was doing and definitely had no immediate plans for the future. We arrived on Friday evening in Mark's van and his friend welcomed us. He informed us that his family was out spending the weekend with some friends and wouldn't be back till Sunday. He then showed us our rooms for the duration of our stay and I leave him chatting animatedly with Mark to wear clothing that is more comfortable.

After dressing, I feel no urge to leave the room and lay back on the bed thinking of nothing in particular. Mark soon comes to get me for dinner and it was a sumptuous affair. Over dinner, Mark tells me about Ted. His friend often added spicy bits of his life Mark forgot and didn't add. From their interactions, I could tell that they were best buddies and my suspicions were soon confirmed. They had been childhood friends and had kept in touch since then. Ted had hit it big as a software engineer and he developed solutions for companies who sought his expertise, in return, they paid him well and he lived comfortably.

He had two kids, Erin and Mina. Erin was overseas studying while Mina, the girl was around my age and out for the weekend with their mother, Lucy. I left for bed as soon as dinner was over. As I climbed up the stairs, I could hear Ted asked Mark in a concerned voice, *"He doesn't look happy, seems pretty sad and somewhat far away. What has he gone through?"*

I am bit far to catch Mark's reply but I do not stop to hear his reply, rather, I plod on and collapse on the bed, pulling the blankets over me. I curl into a ball and watch the night sky through the glass windows.

"A penny for your thoughts," Mark says while snapping his fingers and smiling at me. I let out a deep sigh and pull back

from the well of recollection. *"I have given you time to work it out and it seems that you are finally ready to understand what has caused your failure this time,"* he starts and I listen quietly. Reaching a hand into his overall, he feels around and finally pulls out a picture out of its many pockets. Handing it to me, he says, *"That was your uncle. His nickname Lightening wasn't gotten from his reflexes, it was first because of his quick flashes of anger. In a moment, he could go from being cool to a magma hot rage, despite this; he was always in perfect control. Others might talk of a centre of calm, a rock that keeps other emotions at bay but you and your uncle are different. You have no centre of calm, always angry, but what you do have is a switch, and you can turn it on and off. The stream and flow will always be there, what you have is the control to choose the moments it has a channel to erupt, think about this."*

Patting my shoulder, he stands and walks back the way he came.

Throughout the day, I stay quiet as his words run through my mind. At dinner, I reply to the questions asked politely and retire to bed early. I doze soon however to my surprise.

The next day, Sunday, Ted drove us to church and I enjoyed it.

We got back to see that Ted's family was back. Mark and he both rushed out of the car, all eager to be the first to greet and I walked at a more sedate pace behind them.

There were hugs as I walked into the room and I was introduced to Lucy. She beamed at me and I instantly liked her. Mina had gone upstairs to drop the bags and upon hearing Uncle Mark was around, came rushing back down the stairs and all I could see was a whirlwind of blond hair that threw itself at him. Eventually disengaging from him, she turns around and my heart skips a beat. She smiles as we are introduced and then I excuse myself as the conversation picked up once more.

I return only for dinner and say little. They seemed impressed with the fact that I was a fighter and Mina stole glances at me. Our eyes would meet across the table and I would politely look away, often down at my plate.

We took our leave that evening despite Lucy's protestations and in the van on our way back home, Mark remarks with a knowing grin, *"She likes you."* There is no point asking who and a funny feeling stirs in my heart.

I return to training on Tuesday and the guys are all glad to see me. We do the same things we have been doing and I am surprised when about a week later, Mark announced he had arranged another fight for that Saturday. His reply to my blank stare, *"You are ready, trust me."*

It's the same venue, the same procedure and the same officials, but still things were different. First, the mocking smirk on my opponent's face, second, the crowd didn't chant my name at all, I couldn't hear even a whisper, and I felt nothing. Absolutely nothing, no fear, no anxiety, nothing. Mark didn't say a word, he and the crew prepared me as usual and left the ring after giving me pats on the back.

Ranger Ox smiles at me through his headgear. He has won seven fights by straight knockouts and fourteen others by unanimous decision. Why Mark picked him I could not fathom but he grins wolfishly at me as the bell for the first round rings and homes in on me, like a shark scenting blood.

For the first time in forever, time slows down and everything slows to a walk. All I do is grin and shift on a spot. He unloads a punch with his right and I calmly step into the curve of his arm. His eyes widen fractionally and then growling, he comes even closer and sends in his trademark left hook cum upward slash.

It passes through the space I was in, he stumbles a bit off balance, and the world slows to a complete crawl. *"Now my turn"* I whisper quietly and begin the dance of blood and sweat. His momentum still has him reeling forward and as he comes forward in the delayed time of the void, I unleash a four-two combination on both sides of his face. His breath rushes out in a single whoosh and I step closer as he staggers back, aiming for his body with a one-two combination. He groans as they land, twisting and I push from the tip of my toes, up through my thighs, my chest and finally, the anger roars out and I bend it to my will and it moulds easily into a white-hot molten bubble that hardens my muscles. I connect with an upward jab which lands beside his temple, his feet leaves the ground for the fraction of a second and he crashes to the floor, still and unmoving.

The bout lasted for all of 36 seconds and the crowd went mad with excitement. The announcer doesn't stop booming out in a baritone voice "DID YOU SEE THAT! WHAT A BLOW! OH MY!".

Chapter Eight

A big smile suffuses my face as the countdown begins and the crowd roars in expectation as the numbers increase and he lays unmoving.

Mark winks at me from beside the ring and the crowd explodes as the countdown ends. The referee waves his hands and the bell rings to signify the end of the fight.

The team all jump in, Tim, Drew and Mitch on reaching me, heft me up on their shoulders and begin leading chants of "Boy Hunter", in retrospection. I should have guessed that it would catch on. The arena revs up another octave and goose bumps break out all over my skin. It is an awesome feeling and I feel much bigger than I actually am. Looking around, a memory comes flowing up from the streams of time.

It is memory of a big poster with my uncle who had given birth to my dreams and on whose shoulders I hoped to see the future. I grin as I spot my aunt in the crowd. Her seat is directly beside the ring and I suspect Mike probably had something to do with that. But after further consideration, I begin to think otherwise. She is the wife of a legend after all and had walked in these circles perhaps long before even I was born. She is indeed one very influential aunt as I myself can attest.

The next moments all stand out very clear in my memories. The announcement of the winner, which I was of course, and the sportsmanship hug that was after the medical team had attended to Larry, my opponent. He was groggy at first and not too steady on his feet, but he recovered after a while enough to congratulate me and shared some words.

"Nice going, Kid! I don't think I should call you that however," he adds with a smile, "seeing that you knocked me out cold that is a testament to your ability and points to the fact that you are going far and for that, I am not embarrassed. I see that they have taken to calling you Kid." He says while inclining his head slightly in the direction of the crowd.

I smile in reply. "The accusing fingers lead to my team" and he smiles even more widely.

"Then you have them to thank. Having a nickname such as Kid suggests someone who is small and easily overcomes, attributes that don't come to mind when considering you. You will go far friend and many would be surprised by you." His words though delivered briefly and in a very short span, prove to be true.

Mark wakes me up early the next day by dousing me with a cold bowl of water.

I yelp as I jump out of bed and he doubles over in laughter at my reaction.

I grumble as he continues chuckling and when he recovers enough he says, "Morning sleepyhead, if you assumed you would have a day off perhaps even a week to celebrate your victory, well you thought wrong. The hard work begins now. The champ never stops and if you hope to be one, every minute that goes by must do so with an improvement in your skill and ability."

I wince and squint as he proceeds to switch on every light bulb in my room. I never knew there were so many. He hustles me out of the house in about five minutes and my aunt has a smile on her face as she comes to lock the door behind us. She is still in her night robe and I guess she will head back to bed. I mumble as we head towards Mark's truck. He still has the grin on his face and

I get more suspicious. I am about to enter when he stops me with a hand to my midriff. "Tie this around your waist," he says with a wink holding out a rope and I comply wondering.

Moving to the back of the truck, he attaches the rope to it and comes back around. "You will run with the truck till we reach the gym."

"Oh come on man!" I exclaim in consternation and he grins at me.

"You want to say something?"

I grumble in reply and he laughs out in reply, "I thought so," then he starts the truck and I jog behind it to the gym.

This sets the pace for the following weeks and my training routine actually gets more concentrated. The focus now shifts more on areas concerning style, skill, endurance, technique and power. The sessions are now structured so that each member of the team takes a specialized section and then, there are two general sections.

Invitations for a fight had been pouring in since the last one and Mark had said we should be patient and not rush in picking my next opponent. After some consideration, we decide on Tiger Roo. He has earned a reputation for being a pound for pound fighter and since I had yet to face someone of that style, it was decided it would be the next step in the right direction for my career.

We studied tapes of his recent bouts and analysed the majority of his bouts. He is a danger in close quarters and once he was within range unleashed blows that were often deadly. However, a weakness we noticed was that although he had an amazing engine and reached a peak in every round, he tires easily and could not sustain his attacks. These relative periods of calm were what we banked on. All I just had to do was endure his period of intense attacks.

Mina, along with her mother were in town and came around to visit Mark. They tacitly somehow left us in the house to go visit some friends as Mark put it with a twinkle in his eyes.

I was a perfect gentlemen and Mark had taught me to be extremely polite to ladies, as fighters were perceived not to be so due to their reputation of being unruly. I got to know her better and we had quite a nice time chatting. I served us some refreshments from Mark's fridge and we were munching contentedly when Mark and Lucy got back.

I found myself wishing she didn't have to leave and she somehow managed to steal a kiss on my cheek as they took a leave. Mark caught this with his sharp eyes and I turned beet red as he smothered his laugh. All indication he gave after they left was a cheeky wink and that was all. She gave me her number though.

The day of the fight came and I was confident but not cocky and pretty relaxed, an emotion I was surprised to feel. The fanfare and lights no longer fazed me and I patiently wait for the fight to begin.

Tiger has a mocking smile on his face all through and whispers during the call in, "Hey, I hear they call you Kid, an apt name I guess."

I nod in agreement, and he seems puzzled by my lack of reaction and my cool response.

The bell rings for the first round and he comes at me fast, hard and furious. I find that I face my toughest evading gig yet, as he possesses a wide range of combinations and I have to block furiously as he unleashes a right left combination, a downward jab and right hook that I have to lean to avoid. I feel the wind of the blow as it passes by just a few inches from my cheek and give ground hurriedly as he attempts to get in even closer for his trademark left upwards hook. My arms become heavy and my shoulders begin to ache with the effort of blocking his blows and the power behind them. Blocking a blow does not mean it becomes painless and my forearms are bruised and feel twice their weight.

"Just hold on," Mark calls from the ringside and I do.

Tiger's punches get slower and then panting; he shuffles back a little with hands raised in the guard position.

"Now!" I intone as the same time Mark shouts it.

Weaving to the right, I switch on the rage, yes, now I have a switch and the world slows down to a crawl. Curling a blow from my shoulders, I aim for the right side for his face. He still has enough juice to block with his left but that is what I was hoping. A left hook crashes through his defences and hits him full in the face. He reels backwards and I close the distance. A right left combination to his body forces him to drop his hands to defend and I move in for the kill.

A feint blow sells as a dummy and another blow lands on the underside of his jaw. Jimmying quickly, I shift to the side as his left hook crashes through the space I had been. It would have hit me had I not been on guard. A lesson learnt from my second fight. It is time to end this. I begin a combination I had practiced but never used, a double jab left right, a right hook to the side of the face and gathering my strength unleash an undercutting blow designed to hit the jaw from under with the force snapping back his head. With a gurgle, he stumbles and then crashes to the floor.

I win.

Chapter Nine

It can be said that from this point on, life takes on a new vibrant and more colourful hue. Again, I am hefted up on the shoulders of my team and the whole arena stands giving me an ovation fit for a king and the acclaim to match.

Tiger is stretchered off. I believe he is not as badly hurt as he wanted it to look. I guess after all he had said and all the posturing before the fight, he was ashamed at having lost.

As I am thrown up and down, the last doubts over if this was ever meant to be lifts from my mind, having worked so long and equally hard in training. My first two fights which were losses had dealt heavy blows on my dreams and I had withdrawn into myself, carefully trying to prevent others from coming close and feeling my pain.

Now with two wins on the trot fighters are wishing to take me on as word of me spread. Even now, I can see Mike talking to two men beside the ring and he is gently shaking his head to what one is saying. Guessing they are pitching a potential matchup to him, he will eventually give me the gist when they are done, so I am not overly concerned.

The cameras flash as I am announced as the winner and as was becoming the norm, we return to my corner where my bruises are further examined and cleaned.

Then we head to the changing rooms. My aunt is there already and opening her arms, she engulfs me in a warm hug. "I am proud of you, David." And I grin widely at her.

The celebrations continue late into the night and the guys are all primed up for an all-nighter.

I finally sneak away during a lull and crash in a corner. I am exhausted and in a short while, I am carried off in the arms of Morpheus.

I sleep until late the next morning, as does everyone else. The guys are groggy and Mike sends me out to get eggs. "A breakfast of champions," he tells me with a grin.

I head out into the early morning sun. It feels quite good on my cheeks and walking briskly, I am warmed up in a few minutes. Well, I should say it takes about 20 minutes before I could even get the eggs I had been sent for. I had become something of a celebrity overnight and news of my last fight had spread in the community. I was stopped multiple times to pose for pictures and one little boy asked for my autograph.

I am stunned, as I had not given it much thought although it had occurred to me once or twice. I signed the shirt he had with a flourish and it was quite cool.

At the entrance to the store, two girls also asked me to pose with them and they were quite beautiful. As I shook their hands, one of them presses a slip of paper into my hands and it contains her number and the inscription "call me". I drop the paper in the bin by the racks of the store. The reason, well you can guess, a nice lady with a smile that causes my heart to freeze.

The next couple of weeks were quite fun. It takes a while to get used to being celebrated but once I got used to it, I quietly worked out ways in which it would not overly affect my schedule and my personal life. Also I avoid dark alleys, bars (I don't drink by the way), and outings where ordinary folks would be eager to cause an argument with the hope that it would degenerate into a fight and then they could claim to have beaten a professional fighter in a neighbourhood brawl. Yeah, I know, roll your eyes all you want, but being a fighter ultimately makes you a nice target for bullies and they will swarm you in numbers. All for the bragging rights of having once taken you on.

My aunt advises me not to forget my education and advancing further, perhaps going to college. "Doing that gives an edge and you will feel an accomplishment and a pride in yourself while doing it. All you have to do is pick a course you love and apply yourself while managing your fighting career." Her advice sounds very good and upon further consultations with Mike, we agree that going to college would be a priority.

I begin studying for the entrance exams while also training. My schedule is readjusted accordingly and I still have free time where I can just relax or go visit friends. My income has also been considerable since I began building a reputation and our fees are now respectable, which meant I had quite a bit of savings and also got some cool gadgets for myself to play with and my aunt got most of her domestic appliances upgraded.

My next fight is a ranking fight, meaning it carried points and winning meant a position on the table of ranked challengers to the title. This gave me extra impetus not that I really needed it.

The fight was not as easy as the earlier ones. Mint, as he is called, was much taller than I was and so had a considerable arm length advantage. I was forced to constantly duck his blows while attempting to get in close and I was pounded as a result. We went at it for seven long bouts and in the eighth, I utilized a strategy that Mark and I had developed. It involved acting more tired and worn out than usual while favouring a hand as if were weaker.

Mint took the bait and left his side unprotected, he moved in much closer with the thought that he only had to protect a side.

Grinning, I blocked his first jabs and ducking under a roundhouse swing; I unleash a left right twister to his body and then proceed to pound his face with my reserves.

He falls and I win by knockout. And so, I beat my opponents one after the other, each with differing styles and some with almost no identifiable weakness but I found a way, and so, I move up in the rankings getting closer to challenging the title holder with every win I had under my belt. I keep winning until I am third in the rankings and just a fight and an opponent away from challenging for the title.

However, the opponent I have to face is formidable and has a fearsome reputation. His name alone strikes a chord in the hearts of all who hear it and to me, it serves as a warning that he would be the biggest challenge I would ever face until date. He is known as Danger Bull.

Chapter Ten

It was not all work though. Despite the fight coming up, Mike had passed to me a sense of perspective. At times, we are guilty as humans of concentrating on a single point to the exclusion of all other things. It could be a job or project on which we have our hopes and efforts pinned, but this singular focus eventually makes us lose sight of friends, family, and we forget to smile, to laugh at ourselves, forget it's okay to cry in pain, see failure as weakness and not the lesson that it's meant to be.

Mike taught me perhaps the most important thing in our sessions. "Boxing is a beautiful thing, brutal but still worthy of respect, but at the end, it should not become your life. It should not take the place of your dreams. It adds colour to your life and will give you some of your happiest memories but never forget once in a while, to stand and admire the flowers in the meadow, smell the cold breeze after a rain, watch the laughter of a babe and make friends all around you, never stop living."

I follow his advice and his lead. We never stop living. Several weekends in a row, we would go visit friends and I always looked forward to our visits to

Mike's pal Ted. I got to spend time with Mina and we would sneak away in the afternoons (not sneak, everyone knew where we were) to the garden and would sit on the bench there discussing for hours. We often found many things to talk about and I soon found myself looking forward to our talks. I had been a perfect gentleman since we met and even Mike had told me quite slyly that Ted told him that Lucy was suitably impressed with my conduct. I looked quizzically at him but he only grinned and remarked, "Ladies can be quite confusing." He clamped his mouth shut after that and no amount of glares on my part would make him budge.

At our departure on Sunday, during the usual hugs and cheerful goodbyes, I hung back a little awkwardly after Mina had hugged Mike.

Lucy gave me a push on my back that sent me hurtling towards her. "Come on, at least give her a hug."

Well, I tentatively opened my arms and was pleasantly surprised when she flew into them. "I will miss you, come back soon," she whispers into my ears and I nod. Then she pecks me on the lips and I turn beet red.

Mirthful sounds come from all us and Mike says in an aside to me, "about time".

My head is in the clouds through the drive home and the rest of that day.

My training actually double and then triple as the ranking fight with Danger

Bull draws closer. We analyse tapes of his previous fights, watch his style and combinations and wait for it, but found no tangible weakness. He is a well-rounded fighter, having enough of everything and adapting his style to fit his opponent. He is worth every inch the position he occupies as the second rated fighter in the category.

"You will have to think on your feet for this one Dave. Be wary, don't stress and tire yourself out. Pace yourself and conserve your energy where possible, this might go the full twelve rounds," Mike tells me as we pull into the Rotunda, called the House of Champions. It has seen a host of iconic fights and represents the next stage in my career.

We go through the pre-fight warmup and regulatory procedures. Mike picks an anthem for me. It sounds quite cool as we walk up to the ring.

The arena is massive, sits thousands of fans and a detached part of my mind studies it as we climb into the ring. The crew all crowd around me fitting my gear and Mike kneels in front of me, "Do as we have taught you, be fearless yet wary, deadly and calculating, slippery and tough."

"Oh come on," I groan. "What's with the play on words?"

He grins at me. "I know, still sounds great right, not too goofy," and I smile back at him. "Go get him," he says pulling me to my feet as the referee signals for the fight to begin.

Bull and I exchange acknowledging nods and the bell rings to signal the start of the bout. The first moments instantly confirm our pre-fight analysis. I am facing an intelligent opponent. He is not too close in and not too far away. He stays just at the edges of my reach and able to dart away from my exploratory jabs. We circle each other slowly, exchanging jabs to gauge weaknesses and watching for any slight lowering of guard.

The crowd soon becomes restless with the slow pace at which the fight is progressing and soon begin to chant "Fight, fight, fight!"

Even the commentators get in on the action and Bull slowly smiles as the noise level reaches a crescendo and he explodes forward in a windmill of blows.

I block furiously as he forces me to give ground and I am pushed back towards the ropes.

He increases his speed still and a blow slips through my defences. My head snaps back with the impact and the world wobbles slightly. I am disoriented and a roundhouse to the body knocks out whatever air I had left in my lungs.

The bell rings and the crowd groans in disappointment.

I head towards my corner and am about sitting down when an arm stops me. "This is mine pal, yours is the other side."

Looking around, I am in Bull's corner and trudge across to mine amidst whistles from the crowd.

A splash of cold water and pats soon bring me to full alertness. "Keep it together," Mike, urges me fiercely. "He is faster than you, keep that in mind, and find a way to land your blows without getting severely damaged."

The bell sounds for the next bout and we go at it again. This time, I dart left and right, evading and watching for a chance and it comes. To throw his left hook, he shifts to his right foot to stabilize his centre of gravity and there is a point when his right cannot cover for the space left and then I strike.

Phasing forward, I curl a left fist, which he blocks. It's a combination however and the right hook crashes into his jaw. He staggers backwards and I follow up with my double combinations. He gives ground and then replies with blows of his own. I shift left and right, twisting to get away, a blow catches my left eye and it swells. We trade blows for the next round and each breath becomes fire, agonizing to draw, pain spreads through my muscles and sweat drips out of every pore in rivulets.

Round after round after round, we keep at it and in the seventh, I follow through a right jab and his retaliatory blow catches me right in the face.

I blink as words slur and sift slowly through my brain. Four, five, six.... adrenalin races through my body. I exhibit an acrobatic no handstand Mike had taught me to use in such situations and the crowd roars as I waver slightly but remain on my feet.

The referee confirms my condition and signals for the fight to continue.

"That was a close one," Mike says as he mops my brow. "You have to end it Dave, knock him out, you can't win with points. He has landed more valuable hits on you."

I watch as he comes closer and a memory swims up from the depths. It is from a tape I had watched of my uncle. He had been outmatched but had put everything into one desperate bombardment and he won.

I move forward as Bull comes to meet me halfway. I combust into action, throwing a left right combination, an undercut, a right hook in quick succession and immediately notice something important, Bull is tired. The strain shows on his face as he blocks my blows, his movements are sluggish and summoning my reserves. I begin to pummel his arms, he twists to reduce the onslaught and leaves his left side unprotected, I move in for the kill and time slows down to a crawl.

A roundhouse and a massive smash completely breaks his defence. He wobbles and his arms drop to his sides. Pushing from the tips of my toes, I yell as I unleash a parting shot, aiming for the underside of his jaw. I let go of all rage and push with all of my strength.

His chin compresses with the force of the impact and his eyes roll up into his head. The arena goes quiet as he staggers for a second, then he crumples and falls.

"THE BULL HAS FALLEN!" the announcer screams and I stand, dripping with sweat, exhausted, swollen eyed and victorious.

About the Author

Bill Vincent is no stranger to understanding the power of God. Not only has he spent over twenty years as a Minister with a strong prophetic anointing, he is now also an Apostle and Author with Revival Waves of Glory Ministries in Litchfield, IL. Along with his wife, Tabitha, he, leads a team providing apostolic oversight in all aspects of ministry, including service, personal ministry and Godly character.

Bill offers a wide range of writings and teachings from deliverance, to experiencing presence of God and developing Apostolic cutting edge Church structure. Drawing on the power of the Holy Spirit through years of experience in Revival, Spiritual Sensitivity, and deliverance ministry, Bill now focuses mainly on pursuing the Presence of God and breaking the power of the devil off of people's lives.

His books 48 and counting has since helped many people to overcome the spirits and curses of Satan. For more information or to keep up with Bill's latest releases, please visit www.revivalwavesofgloryministries.com. To contact Bill, feel free to follow him on twitter @revivalwaves.

Recommended Books

By Bill Vincent

Overcoming Obstacles

Glory: Pursuing God's Presence

Defeating the Demonic Realm

Increasing Your Prophetic Gift

Increase Your Anointing

Keys to Receiving Your Miracle

The Supernatural Realm

Waves of Revival

Increase of Revelation and Restoration

The Resurrection Power of God

Discerning Your Call of God

Apostolic Breakthrough

Glory: Increasing God's Presence

Love is Waiting – Don't Let Love Pass You By

The Healing Power of God

Glory: Expanding God's Presence

Receiving Personal Prophecy

Signs and Wonders

Signs and Wonders Revelations

Children Stories

The Rapture

The Secret Place of God's Power

Building a Prototype Church

Breakthrough of Spiritual Strongholds

Glory: Revival Presence of God

Overcoming the Power of Lust

Glory: Kingdom Presence of God

Transitioning to the Prototype Church

The Stronghold of Jezebel

Healing After Divorce

Spiritual Warfare: Complete Collection

Growing In the Prophetic

The Prototype Church: Complete Edition

Faith

The Angry Fighter's Story

Understanding Heaven's Court System

Web Site:

www.revivalwavesofgloryministries.com

9 781684 111510